The Sister
Who Ate
Her Brothers

And Other Gruesome Tales

Jen Campbell

Illustrated by Adam de Souza

T&H

Contents

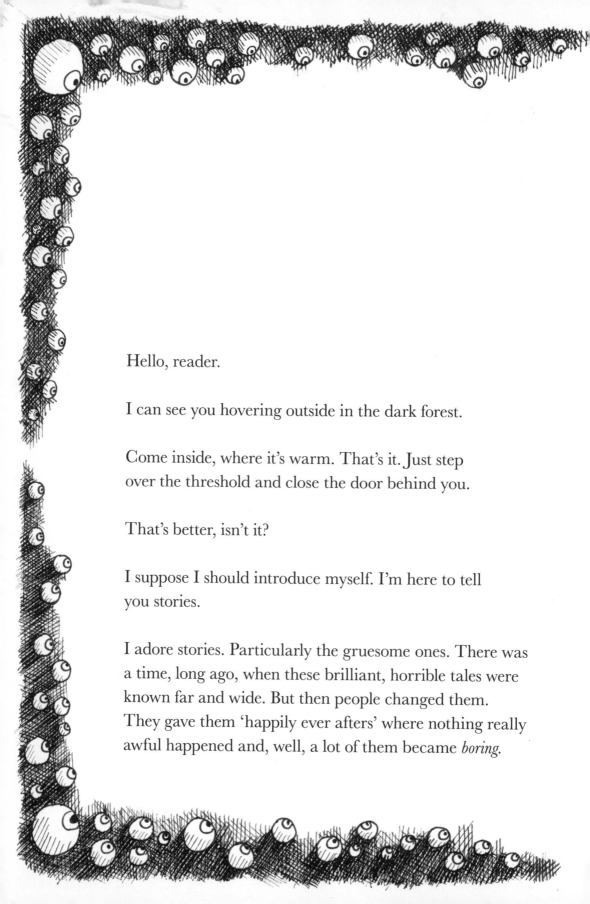

Hello, reader.

I can see you hovering outside in the dark forest.

Come inside, where it's warm. That's it. Just step
over the threshold and close the door behind you.

That's better, isn't it?

I suppose I should introduce myself. I'm here to tell
you stories.

I adore stories. Particularly the gruesome ones. There was
a time, long ago, when these brilliant, horrible tales were
known far and wide. But then people changed them.
They gave them 'happily ever afters' where nothing really
awful happened and, well, a lot of them became *boring*.

So I want to revive those tales of old. The stories where
things hide in the dark. The stories where people eat each
other. The stories where there are holes in the centre of the
earth with terrible things inside.

I am going to tell you some of my favourite tales. I hope you
like them. I hope they please you.

You look a little worried. Don't be.

You say the door has locked itself behind you? Yes, it has a
nasty habit of doing that. Now come and sit down, and listen
to what I have to say.

I'm sure once the stories are over, you'll be able to leave
again.

I said *sit*.

That's better.

Are you comfortable? I hope not.

Oh, we're going to have such fun …

The Sister Who Ate Her Brothers

KOREA

 **T**here once lived a farmer who had three sons but no daughter. His sons brought him joy but he still wished for a girl.

He wished hard.

He wished upon the moon.

He wished for a daughter at any cost – even if she turned out to be half-girl, half-fox.

Nine months later, the farmer's wife gave birth to a girl with a tuft of orange hair. This baby sniffed at every surface; she dug holes in their garden; she growled at the butterflies.

All seemed well.

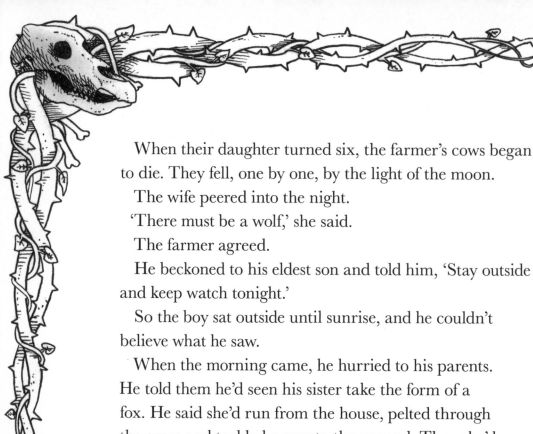

When their daughter turned six, the farmer's cows began to die. They fell, one by one, by the light of the moon.

The wife peered into the night.

'There must be a wolf,' she said.

The farmer agreed.

He beckoned to his eldest son and told him, 'Stay outside and keep watch tonight.'

So the boy sat outside until sunrise, and he couldn't believe what he saw.

When the morning came, he hurried to his parents. He told them he'd seen his sister take the form of a fox. He said she'd run from the house, pelted through the grass and tackled a cow to the ground. Then she'd pulled out its liver and swallowed it whole.

'How dare you!' cried the farmer. 'I've never heard such lies. You must have been dreaming – get out of my house!'

On the second night, the farmer sent his second son to keep watch.

The boy sat beneath a tree, and he couldn't believe what he saw.

When the morning came, he hurried to his parents.
He told them he'd seen his sister take the form of a fox.
He said she'd run from the house, sprinted over the hill
and jumped onto a cow's back. Then she'd wrenched
out its liver and swallowed it whole.

'What nonsense!' cried the farmer. 'You're as mad as
your brother. You're copying his lies. Get out of my house!'

On the third night, the farmer sent his third son to
keep watch.

The boy sat by the cowshed, but he was very, very tired.
He fell into a deep sleep and saw nothing at all.

When the morning came, he hurried to his parents, and
told them a lie. He said he'd been awake all night. He said
he hadn't seen his sister. He said a cow had died of fright
when it had looked at the moon.

'Finally,' his father sighed. 'Here is some truth.'

Meanwhile, the first and second sons wandered down
the road.

Under the midday sun, they came across a Buddhist monk.

They told this monk about their fox sister and asked if he
could help.

'Take these three bottles,' the monk said. 'They will help
you on your quest. Now, go back to your family; go back to
your home.'

The brothers took the three bottles: one red, one white,
one blue.

The strong wind helped them hurry home, but when they
got to the farm, no one was there.

No one, that is, apart from their sister. She was wearing
an apron and held a knife in one hand.

'I've been expecting you.' She grinned. 'I've cooked us
a stew.'

The brothers followed her into the kitchen, for the smell
was irresistible. We must remember they had walked very far,
and they were both very hungry … so we shouldn't judge
them for sitting down and eating that stew.

The three siblings ate.

They chewed and they slurped. They swallowed and
they burped.

CHAPTER 1

When their bellies were full, the two brothers fell asleep.
The house was so quiet, as no one else was home.
The farm was also quiet, as all the cows were gone.
Nothing could disturb them.
Not a thing.

And yet …

The eldest boy awoke in a panic.
His heart was pounding.
Something was very, very wrong.
He turned his head to the side and felt his skin turn to ice.
There was his sister in the form of a fox.
She was bent over the second brother. His liver was in her
hands and there was blood on her chin. In the moonlight,
behind the sofa, he saw the bones of his parents and youngest
brother. The white of their skeletons glowed in the dark.
'I've been saving you for last, big brother,' his little sister
laughed. 'If I eat one more liver, I'll become fully human.
I won't be a fox – I'll be a real little girl.'
The eldest boy ran.
His breath heaved in his chest.
He ran past the dishes, realising what had been in the stew.
He bolted out of the door, speeding into the silver night.

'Not fast enough,' his sister taunted, just three steps behind.

He reached into his bag and pulled out the bottles.

'Take this!' the boy cried, throwing the white one first.

It billowed into smoke and formed a thicket of thorns.

'Not strong enough,' his sister giggled, clawing her way through.

'Take this!' the boy yelled, throwing the blue bottle.

It transformed into a river, blocking her path.

'Not wide enough,' his sister cackled, swimming easily across.

'Then take this!' the boy bellowed, throwing the red bottle.

It burst into flames and consumed the fox whole.

There was no reply this time, as the fire had engulfed her.

His little fox sister was no more than ash.

CHAPTER 2

The Souls Trapped Under the Ocean

IRELAND

 here was once a man who fell in love with a merman. The merman breathed life into his veins and fed him food from the deep.

Every Wednesday, the merman invited the man to his home at the bottom of the sea. It was dusted with salt and glowed in every colour. Lights bobbed in lobster pots along all the walls.

'What do you keep in those pots?' the man signed one day.

'The souls of drowned men and women,' the merman signed back, smiling. 'Eat up! I'll bring you seconds.'

The man hesitated.

He peered more closely at the lights in the pots and shivered.

The merman's house was a cemetery trapped beneath the sea.

'Will you put my soul inside a pot?' the man asked cautiously.

'Not while you're alive,' said the merman calmly. 'But I will once you're dead.'

The man did not know if the merman was joking.

'Now eat your food,' said the merman. 'I made it just for you.'

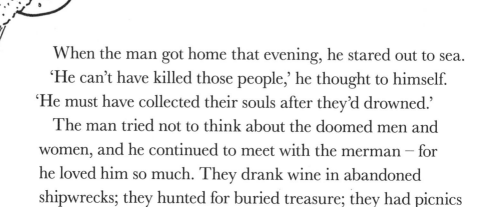

When the man got home that evening, he stared out to sea.

'He can't have killed those people,' he thought to himself.
'He must have collected their souls after they'd drowned.'

The man tried not to think about the doomed men and
women, and he continued to meet with the merman – for
he loved him so much. They drank wine in abandoned
shipwrecks; they hunted for buried treasure; they had picnics
on the beach.

'I wonder what colour your soul is,' the merman mused.
He was staring at him as though he could see his bones.
'Perhaps it's orange like the sun. Or crimson like your heart.'

The man gulped. 'What colour is your soul?'

'Ah, mine is a tapestry!' He cried. 'Tiny pieces of other
people's souls, all stitched together.' He reached down and
picked up fragments of shells and arranged them across the
sand. 'It's the only way to live, my love. It's the only way
to breathe.'

Over the next few weeks, villagers began to die.

At first, the man thought it was an accident: people
walking along the beach at night, caught out by the tide.
Their lifeless bodies washed up in the morning, their lungs
filled with the sea.

But as more souls were added to the merman's underwater
house, the man became afraid. He stroked the souls through
the bars. One cherry light was the soul of the baker.
One mustard light was the soul of the lighthouse keeper.

Many of these people had been his friends. He needed to set them free.

When the merman was out catching mackerel, the man swam to the merman's study and pulled an old key from a drawer. He slid it into the lock of a lobster pot and set a blue soul free.

The light of the soul blinked gratefully.

The man worked quickly.

Soon, souls were swimming all around him. An amber soul. A pink one. A silver soul. An emerald one. They circled him like traffic lights.

'Go,' the man signed, ushering them out. 'Be free!'

The souls darted like fish into the dark, dark ocean, and the man breathed a sigh of relief.

The man waited for the merman to return, wondering how angry he would be. But the clock ticked, and night fell, and the merman did not come home. The man searched the sea for hours, weaving between the rocks and when there was still no sign, he swam wearily to shore.

The man's heart broke in two when he found the merman on the sand.

The merman's skin had lost its colours – all life drained from his face. For the borrowed souls that had kept him alive had swum so far away.

The House That Was Filled With Ghosts

JAPAN

here once lived a woman who made the best tea in the land. Every day it tasted of something different. Sometimes it tasted of syrup pears, on other days it smelled of roasted almonds, and occasionally it had a hint of sweet red bean paste. Those who drank it said it reminded them of dreams they'd had as children. The woman's father was extremely proud of her talent, and he liked to show off to his clients by asking her to make tea whenever he had important meetings. Consequently, many businessmen fell in love with her, and some asked for her hand in marriage. But she always shook her head. She had not yet met the person she wanted to spend her life with.

Then, one day, when she was walking through the fire-red maple trees, she did meet someone. It was her father's gardener, who was new to their household. She introduced herself and the pair spent the afternoon talking. They shared tea that tasted of autumn, and neither noticed when night slinked across the sky.

The woman and the gardener fell deeply in love,
but her father would not consent to their marriage.

'He is poor!' her father scolded. 'You can do better
than that.'

The woman and the gardener sighed; they did not care
about money.

'Please, sir,' said the gardener. 'What if I can find a huge
house for your daughter? A house with a thousand rooms?'

The father laughed. 'You will never be able to afford such
a place.'

'But if I found one,' he went on, 'would you let us marry?'

The father paused. He knew the gardener would never be
able to afford a house with a thousand rooms. So he nodded,
smirking. 'If you ever live in a house with a thousand rooms,
you may marry my daughter.'

CHAPTER 3

It just so happened that the gardener did know of a house with a thousand rooms. It sat on top of a mountain, surrounded by giant trees. Inside, there were rooms filled with many different things. One room was filled with music. Another was filled with footsteps. One room was filled with a silence so loud that if you screamed into it, you would hear nothing at all. The house was also said to be full of ghosts, and it was because of this that no one lived there. It was owned by a prince who refused to enter it. In fact, no one had stayed there for hundreds of years.

The gardener went to visit the prince.

'Your highness.' He bowed. 'I have a request.'

The prince raised an eyebrow. He did not like requests.

'My wife and I would like to live in your house with a thousand rooms.'

The prince snorted. 'And why should I let you do that?'

'Because we can get rid of the ghosts,' said the gardener, who had no idea if this was true. 'We will scare them away and then you will have your house back.'

Even though the prince lived in a magnificent castle, it annoyed him that he could not visit his other house. So, reluctantly, he gave the gardener the keys.

Now the woman's father had to let them marry.

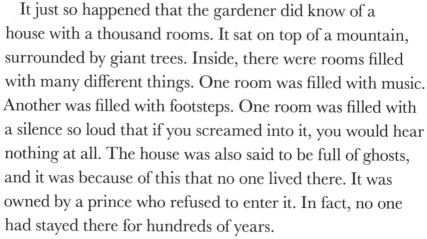

Autumn had given way to winter, and it was a struggle
to reach the top of the mountain to get to their new home.
The wild snow came up to their knees, and the horses
carrying their possessions were scared by the house's
shadow and kept trying to run away.

The gardener hadn't told his new wife about the ghosts
because he didn't want to frighten her. When they pushed
open the huge front door, the house rumbled with hunger.

'What a strange place,' the woman whispered, tiptoeing
down the hall lined with hand-shaped candlesticks, each
one holding a different coloured flame.

They could have spent years exploring the house.
The rooms seemed to multiply. There was a room with
suitcases addressed to non-existent places, a basement full
of tunnels that disappeared into nothing, and the taps
trickled with an odd laughter.

The woman loved the house, even though it was far away
from the rest of the world. Her husband had to leave in the
middle of the night to get to work on time. He set off just
after midnight, and she watched him sleepily as he battled
down the mountain. Unable to get back to sleep, she brewed
some tea in one of the many kitchens and inhaled its scent of
snow. The house watched as she waltzed down the corridors,
peered into endless cupboards and sang up the stairs.

When her husband left for work on the
third night, something changed. A wind
crept in from the west and wound its way
inside the house. It lifted the rugs and rattled
the paintings. The woman hurried downstairs to
see what was wrong.

Out of the darkness, three candles appeared.

At first, she thought they were hanging in the air, but
as they glided closer she saw that they were held by three
monks in white cloaks. She could not see their faces. They
stomped nearer and then surrounded her. Most people would
have screamed. Most people would have fled. But this woman
was not like most people.

She peered at the monks, intrigued.

'Would you like some tea?' She smiled. 'It's a cold,
cold night.'

So she gave the monks some tea. It tasted of sweet miso
and plum blossom. Then she opened the door to one of the
dusty ballrooms, turned on the gramophone, and the four of
them danced until the sun rose. The monks' candles flickered,
the woman giggled, and the ancient house was pleased.

When her husband left for work on the fourth night,
another wind invited its way into the house. This time it
came from the east. It shook the cutlery drawers and knocked
books off the shelves. The woman hurried downstairs to see
what was wrong.

Out of the darkness, three candles appeared. At first, she thought they were hanging in the air, but as they crept closer she saw that they were held by three monks in yellow cloaks. She could not see their faces. They slid nearer and surrounded her. Most people would have yelled. Most people would have run. But this woman was not like most people.

'Would you like some tea?' She beamed. 'It's so frosty outside.'

So she gave the monks some tea. It tasted of yuzu and honey. Then she opened the door to a room full of broken mirrors, turned on the gramophone, and the four of them danced until the morning birds sang. The monks' candles made constellations on the silver surfaces, and the house watched it all, feeling snug and content.

When the husband left for work on the fifth night, a third wind made its way into the house. This time it came from the south. It peeled back the wallpaper and bounced off the ceiling. The woman hurried downstairs to see what was wrong.

Out of the darkness, three candles appeared. At first, she thought they were hanging in the air, but as they crept closer she saw that they were held by three monks in black cloaks. She could not see their faces. They slithered nearer and surrounded her. Most people would have cried. Most people would have scarpered. But this woman was not like most people.

'Would you like some tea?' she sang. 'It's bitter outside.'

So she gave the monks some tea. It tasted of liquorice and midnight treacle. Then she opened the door into the vanilla-smelling library, turned on the gramophone, and the four of them danced until morning arrived. The monks' candles winked and the house watched them happily. Its soul was full of warmth, for it finally felt loved.

When the gardener came home that day, he found his wife fast asleep on a pile of old books.

'What are you doing?' He grinned. 'Did you have a party?'

The woman laughed and brewed them both tea. She told him all about the ghostly monks she had danced with and how the house had come alive all around her.

'I don't think those ghosts are going to come back,' she sighed. 'Which is a shame, in many ways.'

The gardener was so proud of his wonderful wife. When he told the prince that she had cleaned his house of ghosts, the prince was so amazed that he asked if the gardener and his wife would like to live there forever. The gardener could tend to the grounds, and his wife could take care of the house.

'On one condition,' said the prince merrily. 'Whenever I come to visit, I would like your brave wife to make me a delicious cup of tea.'

CHAPTER 4

The Boy Who Tricked a Troll

NORWAY

I n a village next to the deepest forest, where the trees scraped the sky and their roots strangled the earth, everyone knew you should be home before dark.

If you weren't home by then, you might never return.

Many had gone missing.

But one boy didn't care.

This boy loved the dark. He adored running through it, he cherished jumping over it. He took pleasure in the way that the dark tickled his chin and coaxed him into the shadows.

One night, he was scampering through the undergrowth, collecting as many mushrooms as he could carry. Soon his rucksack was full, so he stuffed the rest into a small bag fastened around his waist. There were purple mushrooms and green mushrooms, striped ones and spiky ones. There were even a few that glowed in the dark.

It was those that gave the boy away.

A troll the size of a tree saw the boy's face all lit up in
the glow of the mushrooms, and he thundered over to him,
grabbing him by the throat.

'Give me those mushrooms!' the troll bellowed. 'Give them
to me now, or I'll feed you to the night!'

The boy gulped. 'Let's share them,' he said, trying to sound
calm. 'For there are hundreds, and I am the best cook in the land.
I promise these will be the best mushrooms you've ever had!'

The troll scowled and dropped the boy.

'I will be the judge of that,' he spat. 'Now, cook!'

The boy cooked. He pulled a frying pan from his rucksack, and
he fried the mushrooms in butter and garlic. The smell floated
across the forest, waking the bears and tempting the wolves.

The boy balanced on a large toadstool and he served their
food on a fallen log.

'Here you go,' he said, grinning. 'Tuck in!'

The boy was right: the mushrooms were delicious.
They devoured as many as they could, but there were
still yet more to eat.

'I want them all,' groaned the troll. 'But I am full.'

'I am full, too,' said the boy. 'But I have a plan. If we cut
our stomachs open and let the food fall out, we'll have more
room inside us, and then we can eat whatever we want.'

The troll was suspicious. 'That sounds dangerous,' he said.
'You do it first and I'll watch. If you don't, I'll feed you to
the night.'

The boy obeyed. He picked up his knife and cut across his stomach. However, he didn't cut his skin. He was still wearing the small bag around his waist. So, instead of hurting himself, he tore across the bag's fabric and all the mushrooms inside it tumbled to the floor.

'See!' said the boy. 'It didn't hurt at all, and now my stomach is empty!'

The troll applauded. 'What a good plan!' he cried, and he picked up his knife. He dragged the blade across his own stomach, but of course this was a terrible idea.

The troll howled. He glanced down in astonishment, watching his guts tumbling out of his body. They landed with a wet splash upon the grass below.

'Tricked you!' the boy giggled, running off into the dark.

The troll yelled: 'Come back here, so I can feed you to the night!' But when he tried to get to his feet, more of his insides fell out. The troll crashed into the bushes and sank into the mud.

Then the bears and wolves who had smelled those delicious mushrooms descended upon the troll and ate till they were full.

The Daughter Who Loved a Skeleton

NIGERIA

O nce there was a young woman who decided she wanted to marry. She picked up a pencil and drew a picture of a man, then she took this to her parents.

'This is the person I want,' she said. 'I will accept nobody else.'

Her parents tried to protest but the young woman insisted. She did not care if this man was kind. She did not care if this man was good. She just wanted a man who looked exactly like her drawing. To her, this man was the most beautiful being she had ever seen. So her parents made copies of her picture and pinned them all over town.

They waited, and they waited, but no men came – for there was no one in the kingdom who looked like that.

THE DAUGHTER WHO LOVED A SKELETON

In the coming weeks, news of this seeped out of the world of the living and into the world of the dead. A copy of the daughter's drawing flew past the window of an ancient castle, where a skeleton lived. He reached out a hand and grabbed it.

'Well,' he said, studying it closely. 'I think I can manage that.'

The skeleton told his mother he was going out, then he raided the local graveyard and found ears that matched the drawing. In another coffin, he found some legs. He scooped up a pair of eyeballs and cherry-picked a smile. Then he waltzed into the world of the living, and walked up to the daughter's house, looking the perfect image of her picture.

'This is so exciting!' cried the daughter. 'We should get married right now!'

The skeleton smiled. 'I'd like you to meet my mother first. Pack a suitcase – it's quite far.'

The daughter packed in a hurry, leaving a note for her parents.

'How will we get to your house?' she asked. 'Will we take a bus?'

The skeleton grinned. 'No, we'll take a cloud.'

CHAPTER 5

The daughter blinked and the skeleton reached up to grab a storm cloud from the sky. He jumped on top of it and pulled the daughter up after him, then he summoned a mighty gale to blow them to his home.

The daughter did not know what to say. She clung to the edge of the cloud, which soaked her to her bones. The wind got under her skin and made a home there. Droplets of rain froze on her eyelashes, and the sky all around them turned an ominous grey.

The cloud hit a pocket of air and bumped its way into the world of the dead. The daughter began to feel strange – as if half of the air had left her lungs, and half of her blood had left her body.

'Welcome to my kingdom,' said the skeleton, shaking off his borrowed body parts. He dropped these into the graveyard as they flew overhead. 'This is my home.'

A castle loomed in front of them. At first, the daughter thought it was made of pearls, but as they got closer she realised it was made of teeth. Indeed, as they swooped down in front of it, the walls of the castle started muttering. They whispered harsh words she couldn't quite hear.

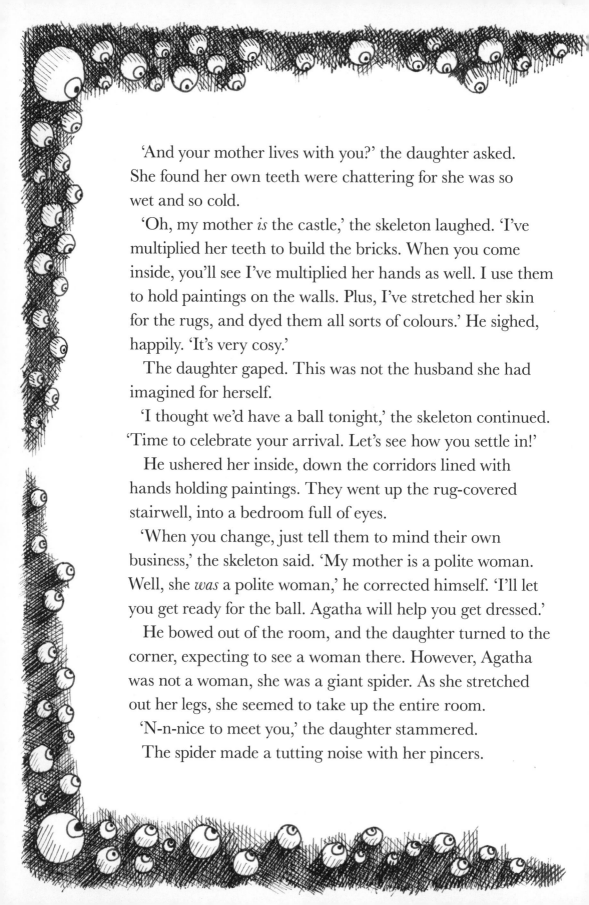

'And your mother lives with you?' the daughter asked. She found her own teeth were chattering for she was so wet and so cold.

'Oh, my mother *is* the castle,' the skeleton laughed. 'I've multiplied her teeth to build the bricks. When you come inside, you'll see I've multiplied her hands as well. I use them to hold paintings on the walls. Plus, I've stretched her skin for the rugs, and dyed them all sorts of colours.' He sighed, happily. 'It's very cosy.'

The daughter gaped. This was not the husband she had imagined for herself.

'I thought we'd have a ball tonight,' the skeleton continued. 'Time to celebrate your arrival. Let's see how you settle in!'

He ushered her inside, down the corridors lined with hands holding paintings. They went up the rug-covered stairwell, into a bedroom full of eyes.

'When you change, just tell them to mind their own business,' the skeleton said. 'My mother is a polite woman. Well, she *was* a polite woman,' he corrected himself. 'I'll let you get ready for the ball. Agatha will help you get dressed.'

He bowed out of the room, and the daughter turned to the corner, expecting to see a woman there. However, Agatha was not a woman, she was a giant spider. As she stretched out her legs, she seemed to take up the entire room.

'N-n-nice to meet you,' the daughter stammered.

The spider made a tutting noise with her pincers.

She pushed the daughter into the bathroom and under a
cold shower. After that, the spider stuffed her into an ancient
wedding dress hemmed with tattered lace, and the daughter
fell into a chair in front of the dressing table. Agatha pushed
and pulled at her hair and dabbed her face with make-up.
All the while, the eyes dotted around the room never once
left the daughter's face.

In the cobwebbed ballroom, the skeleton climbed onto a podium. 'Welcome, everyone!' he boomed. 'I have asked you to gather here today to meet the woman I wish to marry. She called to me from the world of the living, and I have presented her to my mother.' The skeleton paused here, looking up at the fleshy ceiling. 'My mother will decide if this woman is good enough to take my hand. In the meantime, let us feast and dance!'

The room was full of the strangest creatures. Other skeletons, yes, but not just human ones. Scattered across the dancefloor were the skeletons of aardvarks and elephants, rhinos and crocodiles.

'Canapé?' asked the skeleton, waving a plate of food in front of the daughter. She was very hungry, so she reached out a hand but then stopped. The plate was covered in rotting meat.

She wrinkled her nose.

'No, thank you,' she said.

The skeleton frowned. 'If you refuse to eat, my mother will not be happy.'

He disappeared with the canapés, offering them to his other guests, before coming back with another tray.

'Wine?' the skeleton asked, holding out a glass. The daughter was very thirsty, so she reached out a hand but then stopped. The glass was full of clotted blood.

She felt a little sick.

'No, thank you,' she said.

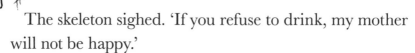

The skeleton sighed. 'If you refuse to drink, my mother will not be happy.'

He vanished with the tray, weaving between his guests, before coming back to her once again.

'Shall we dance?' he asked smoothly. Nearby, Agatha started to play a string quartet.

The skeleton steered the daughter into the middle of the room and the guests parted to let them through. She did not know how to dance, so she let him lead. But as her feet were dragged across the floor, she could somehow feel that more blood was evaporating from her body, and even more air was draining from her lungs. The daughter closed her eyes. She knew that if she stayed in this world much longer, she would definitely end up dead. She took a shallow breath and pushed the skeleton away from her.

'I want to stop this,' the daughter said. 'I want to stop this right now!'

Her voice echoed around the room.

The music fizzled and died.

The skeleton looked embarrassed.

He stamped his foot. 'If you refuse to dance, my mother will not be happy.'

The castle began to grumble. The sound seemed to come up from the basement. The wallpaper peeled back to reveal more eyes in the walls.

Indeed, the skeleton's mother was not happy.

'Now, now, Mother,' the skeleton spoke calmly. 'I'm sure this woman is worthy of my hand.'

But the castle did not think so, and the daughter was glad.

She realised what she had to do.

She raced around the room, breaking all the glasses she could reach. She knocked the chairs sideways and pushed the tables to the floor.

The castle started to scream.

It was a gut-wrenching, foul scream that poisoned the air.

The daughter fled.

The rugs lifted from the floor – huge tongues, trying to trip her up. As she pelted into the hall, the hands dropped their paintings and chased after her too. The teeth on the outside of the castle were chattering so loudly. she felt as if she was trapped inside a giant's skull.

The front door wasn't far, but the daughter didn't know if she would make it. There was hardly any air left inside her lungs.

Just as she reached out to grab the doorhandle, something seized her from behind, clamping her shoulders. The daughter wilted. She knew she had no energy left to fight her way out.

47

'Climb on,' came a whisper, and eight arms lifted her body onto the back of a huge spider. It seemed Agatha had had enough of this old place, too.

They both heaved the front door open.

The castle screamed even louder.

The daughter and the spider tumbled into the night – and just in time. As Agatha hurried down the garden path, the daughter turned her neck to see the door of the castle stretching into a colossal mouth. All the teeth on the outside sharpened into fangs. The castle shrieked and all its windows shattered. Its wailing became an angry wind that zigzagged across the deadened sky.

'Hold on!' Agatha called, and she used this wind to lift them up onto a storm cloud. The pair of them held on tight as it whisked them far away.

The daughter collapsed on Agatha's back, completely exhausted.

She listened to her own heartbeat as Agatha navigated the mists, flying over the graveyards of the world of the dead. And as they bumped their way back into the world of the living, the daughter felt brilliant cold air flooding back into her lungs.

The Princess Who Ruled the Sea

INUIT

In the purple-blue north where the snow never melts, an ice king summoned suitors for his daughter.

Tall men.

Short men.

Wise men.

Strong men.

His daughter watched the suitors zigzagging along the cliffs, battling the sea wind to line up beneath her window. She sighed, for she did not want to marry any of them.

'I'd rather marry you,' she said to her dog.

Her dog barked in agreement.

Over their midnight feast, the king asked his daughter, 'Have you picked a husband?'

She smiled, sipping crowberry juice. 'I have.'

'Is he handsome and wise?'

'He is furry and kind.'

'Is he princely and royal?'

'He is playful and loyal.'

The king shrugged and said, 'My princess, whomever you have chosen will be good enough for me.'

But this was not true, for the king had an anger that lived deep inside him, and when he discovered that his daughter wanted to marry a dog, he flew into a rage. He smashed the glass walls of their palace, dragged his daughter to the frosty beach and tossed her onto his biggest ship.

The sea muttered to itself as they sailed out into the dark waters.

The king grabbed his daughter and dangled her over the side of the boat, her blue velvet cape cocooning around her. 'If you do not agree to marry a prince,' he spat, 'I will throw you into the sea!'

But his daughter was not afraid, for she loved the sea. She breathed in deeply, tasting salt on her tongue.

'I do not want to marry any of those men,' she said, her eyes the colour of seaweed.

'So be it!' the king roared and let go of her.

The princess tried to cling to the side of the ship, but the king grabbed an axe and cut off her fingers one by one, and so the princess

tumbled

into the waves.

At first, she found it hard to see. The water hugged her bones, and the current combed her hair. Her cape snaked down her body and wrapped itself around her legs. So now the princess had a tail. Her fingers floated down beside her and, slowly, they began to transform. Her little fingers turned into skeleton shrimps. The next fingers became seals. The others turned into killer whales, Greenland sharks and narwhals.

She grinned as the sea sang its songs to her, cradling her in its arms. Then she flicked her tail and set off to explore this underwater kingdom, this blue-green world.

In time, the princess became a goddess of the deep: a ruler of tides and storms.

CHAPTER 7

The Husband Who Cheated Death

EGYPT

There was once a man who felt very ill, so he gathered his family and friends around him.

'Dearest wife,' he said, taking her hand. 'Will you please put on your wedding dress? Will you wear your silver shoes? And will you put gold in your hair?'

'Of course,' she said, smiling sadly, and she began to do all of these things at once. 'Is this because you want to remember our wedding day before you die?'

'No,' said the husband slyly. 'It is because they say that Death takes the best of us. So I'm hoping he will take you instead.'

And, with that, Death appeared and whisked the wife away.

The Adults Who Lost Their Organs

GERMANY

here were once three butchers who were called away to war. It was their job to operate on soldiers, to sew wounds and to bandage limbs. They called themselves the Butcher Surgeons. The first was the height of two broomsticks. The second was the daughter of a witch. The third had a beard shaped like a tree.

One night, after a particularly violent battle, the Butcher Surgeons were looking for somewhere to sleep. They swaggered into a small village and knocked on the door of an inn.

'We want a room.' They grinned. 'But we don't have any money.'

The innkeeper laughed nastily. 'Then you can sleep on the streets! You can't stay here.'

'Ahhh, but what about a different kind of payment?' They leaned over the threshold. 'What about a magic trick?'

'Magic?' the innkeeper snorted. 'There's no such thing!'

The Butcher Surgeons looked at him with pity.

CHAPTER 8

'Here's what we propose,' said the first. 'We will each cut off a body part.'

'You will keep those body parts safe overnight,' said the second.

'Then, in the morning, we will reattach those body parts,' said the third.

'And if we are unable to do so,' they chorused, 'we will come back next week and pay you double.'

The innkeeper paused. Surely this was easy money? No one could cut off parts of their body and reattach them again.

'Okay,' he said, holding out a silver plate. 'Give them to me.'

The first Butcher Surgeon cut off a hand and handed it over.

The second pulled out an eye and rolled it onto the plate.

The third reached inside his chest and pulled out his heart. It twitched red and purple in the fading evening light.

The innkeeper didn't know what to say. He held the plate at arm's length, invited them inside and ushered them into the biggest room. After all, when their magic trick failed and they had to pay double, he wanted them to pay for the most expensive room.

Then he raced to the kitchen, balancing the hand and the eyeball and the heart. He thrust them at the cook, shouting, 'Keep these safe, do you hear?'

The cook did hear, but he didn't care. He put the body parts to one side and promptly forgot about them.

Soon enough, the kitchen cat jumped
onto the counter. She tiptoed around the plate
and gave the human flesh a sniff. The cat thought
it smelled delicious, so she opened her mouth wide.
She swallowed the eye, then she gobbled the hand and,
finally, she chewed the heart delicately until all of it
was gone.

When the cook realised what had happened, he panicked.
He didn't want to lose his job, so he raced into the streets
with his sharpest knife. He cornered a thief and cut off his
hand. He chased the kitchen cat and took out one of her
eyes. He grabbed a pig from the local farm and pulled
out its heart.

He placed these glistening body parts on the silver plate,
then put them in the fridge out of harm's reach.

In the morning, the well-rested Butcher Surgeons came
down for breakfast, and the innkeeper presented them
with the silver plate.

'Let's see this magic then,' he sneered, still sure
it was a lie.

The Butcher Surgeons smiled.

The first sewed the hand back on with fine golden thread.

59

The second tossed the eyeball into the air and caught
it in her socket.

The third hugged the heart gratefully and rammed
it back inside his chest.

'Thanks for your hospitality,' they said, bowing. 'Now we'll
be on our way.'

But it was a curious thing. The Butcher Surgeons didn't
feel quite like themselves that day. The first felt their hand
twitching, longing to steal coins. The second, when night fell,
could now see in the dark. The third had the strongest urge
to roll around in mud.

'Shall we have mice for dinner?' asked the second Butcher
Surgeon. 'I could catch some for us.'

'I could steal some money and buy us something better,'
said the first.

'Why go hunting or stealing, when we could just eat scraps?'
said the third, who was hunting for vegetable peelings in a
nearby bin.

'Oh dear!' said the first.

'Meow!' said the second.

'Oink!' said the third.

Realising they had been tricked, they hurried back to
the inn. They hammered on the door, calling out for their
body parts, but there was nothing that could be done.

All that was waiting for them was a very full cat, an
apologetic cook and an innkeeper who now definitely
believed in magic.

The Kingdoms at the Centre of the Earth

RUSSIA

nce there was a queen who was worried her son and daughter would never marry, so she went to a wise man in the west.

'Give this ring to your son,' he told the queen. 'Tell him that he must marry whomever the ring fits.'

'What about my daughter?' she asked. 'Do you have a ring for her?'

'Oh, don't worry about her.' He grinned. 'Your daughter will be fine.'

So the queen gave the ring to her son. It was set with an onyx stone. The gem was so dark that when her son looked into it, he felt as if he was falling into a deep, deep well.

'You must travel the world,' the queen said, stroking her son's cheek. 'Make every person try it on. When you find someone whose hand fits perfectly, bring them home.'

So the son left their castle and set out on his travels, leaving his mother and sister behind. He trekked through the snow. He crossed deserts and wetlands. He sailed monster-filled seas and stomped over bleak Arctic plains. But the ring did not fit any person he met.

After many years, the son returned, feeling bitter and angry. He'd stared at the ring for so long that his eyes matched its colour.

'Don't be grumpy,' his sister sighed. 'What's so special about this ring, anyway?' And before her brother could reply, she had taken it from him and slipped it onto her finger.

The ring snapped into place. It was the perfect fit.

She laughed nervously. 'I suppose this means that you have to marry me.'

'But of course!' cried the brother, jumping to his feet. 'We must marry quickly! You shall be my faithful wife!'

'I … I was joking,' she stammered, trying to pull away from him. 'You can't marry me. I'm your sister!'

'I don't care!' the brother replied, his eyes as deep as caves. 'I am your future king. You will do as I say!'

The sister did not know what to do, so she hurried to a wise woman in the east and explained her troubles.

'Sew four dolls,' the woman said calmly. 'Put each of them in a corner of the room. Then wait.'

'Wait for what?' the sister asked.

'Just wait.'

The sister ran back home and picked up a needle and thread. She made four dolls from old dresses and fruit peelings, and she stuffed them with straw. Then she put them in the shadowed corners of her bedroom and sat in the middle of the floor, listening to her brother marching through the castle.

'Sister!' he yelled. 'You must try on your wedding dress!'

She closed her eyes tight, her heart hammering, hammering, hammering.

She waited and she waited …

Then out of the dark came this haunting song:

> 'Cuckoo, he takes his sister.
> Cuckoo, for a wife!
> Cuckoo, earth open wide.
> Cuckoo sister, fall inside!'

The sister's bedroom began to shake and shatter. She screamed, opening her eyes just in time to see the four dolls laughing and racing towards her. She tried to scramble to her feet, but the floor had disappeared and so she plummeted

down
down
down.

Down to the centre of the earth.

The sister landed with a bump.

She found herself in a sea-blue kingdom. There were peacocks as tall as houses, and everything smelled of lavender. The huge birds flapped their tail feathers angrily, so she ran, tumbling into a river. She was dragged downstream and washed up on the shores of an orange kingdom.

Here there were tigers with volcanoes in their mouths, so she scampered sideways, rushing into a yellow kingdom with bees the size of stars. She ran from there into a green kingdom that gurgled, a red kingdom that roared, and a pink kingdom that chewed her up and spat her out into a silver kingdom. She tiptoed across its tightrope of knives … And then … then there was darkness.

The sister had found the night kingdom.

Things she couldn't see pulled at her hair and trod on her toes.

She felt her way past a row of out-of-tune pianos, which were playing by themselves.

She inched forwards, her arms outstretched, until she felt the sandpaper skin of trees. This was a night forest. She crept further, deep into the belly of the woods, where she was sure the dark would eat her.

CHAPTER 9

'Cuckoo!'

Her hands touched the walls of a house.

She blinked, her eyes becoming accustomed to the night.

This was a house made of scraps: camera lenses and coat
hangers, blackbird feathers and broken umbrellas. The
sister's fingers shook as she fumbled for the door knocker.
Bang, bang, bang! And somewhere inside, a light flicked on.

'Cuckoo, earth open wide.

Cuckoo sister, fall inside!'

The door cracked open, and the sister froze.

She wanted to run but she couldn't.

She wanted to scream but she'd forgotten how.

The woman behind the door looked just like her. It was like staring into a grimy mirror, except this woman's eyes were as deep as caves. She smiled and the sister could hear the laughter of the dolls she had made back home.

'I've been expecting you.' The woman beamed, grabbing her by the wrist.

The sister was pulled over the threshold. As she stumbled inside, the house began to shrink. The dark walls and crooked ceiling tumbled towards them both in a rush of noise and feathers.

'Cuckoo! Cuckoo!'

And they were back in the sister's room.

'Sister! I told you, you must try on your wedding dress!'
Her brother crashed into the room, his face full of fury.
'You have to –'

He stopped. He blinked.

He did not know what to think.

Two women stood before him. They were the same in
every way, except …

'You have my eyes,' the brother gasped.

'I do,' the woman murmured. She let go of the sister's
wrist and glided towards him. As she got closer, she appeared
to grow taller. She towered above him and he was unable to
look away.

'Who are you?' the brother asked, mesmerised.

'We should get married,' the woman said, sliding an arm
around his waist.

'Y-yes.' He blinked rapidly, as sweat formed on his upper
lip. 'Yes! Sister, give me back my ring!'

Relief flooded through his sister as she pulled the onyx
ring from her hand and threw it across the room.

The woman caught it.

She slid it onto her finger, and it snapped into place.

It was the perfect fit – of course it was.

And so the sister was free.

The woman giggled wickedly, ushering the brother out
of the room and across the castle.

As she watched them go, the sister noticed how this woman moved just like a doll.

'Cuckoo! Cuckoo!'

A doll with eyes so deep they could swallow a man whole.

CHAPTER 10

The Wife Who Could Remove Her Head

EL SALVADOR

O nce there was a woman who was a witch. She didn't tell her husband about her magic powers, because he wasn't a very nice man, and she enjoyed using spells to go off on her own adventures.

Every night, she used a spell to remove her head from her body. Then her head was free to zoom all around the world. She dived into oceans. She visited outer space. She flew with firebirds and she ate with vampires.

One night, a neighbour saw the witch's head flying out of the window. He raced next door to tell the husband.

'Wake up! Wake up!' he yelled. 'Your wife has run away!'

'Don't be silly,' the husband yawned. 'She's right here beside me.'

He patted the body lying next to him, but the neighbour pulled back the covers to show him she had no head.

'What is this witchcraft?' the husband cried, leaping out of bed.

'You must rub salt along her neckline,' the neighbour told him. 'That will stop her evil ways. That will put you in control.'

So the husband did as the neighbour said. He rubbed salt along his wife's neckline, then he pretended to be asleep and waited for her to return.

As the sun peered over the horizon, his wife's head drifted in through the open window. She was exhausted but happy from dancing with the clouds. Her head dropped down onto her shoulders … and she frowned. Something was wrong. She could not attach her head to her body.

'Aha!' the husband shrieked. 'I have broken your wicked spell!'

The wife rolled her eyes.

'How tiresome,' she said. 'I suppose I'll have to live on you instead.'

Her head hopped over to his shoulder and she attached herself there.

'That wasn't what I had in mind.' The husband scowled.

'Tough,' said the wife. 'You've brought this upon yourself.'

So, during the day, the wife's head was attached to her husband's shoulder, and during the night she detached herself and zoomed out of the window to continue having adventures.

The husband did not enjoy this. One night when his wife's head was gone, he went into the garden and pulled a mammee tree from the ground.

He dragged it into their house and hid it in their bed. He arranged the branches to look like arms, and he chopped off the top so it looked like a neck.

When morning came, the wife's head came back home and she attached herself to the wood, thinking it was her husband asleep in the bed. She drifted off to sleep and when she woke a few hours later, she realised she had turned into a tree.

'Aha!' the husband cried triumphantly. He dragged his wife into the garden to plant her in the soil. 'Now I have you caught, and you must do as I say!'

'Oh, you haven't caught me,' said the wife with a smile.

Indeed, the husband had not – for it is difficult to catch a
witch. Much to the husband's annoyance, the wife enjoyed
being a tree. She stretched her twig-limbs in the sun, and
whenever she was hungry she ate the fruit growing out of
her skin.

Then, when she was ready, she produced hundreds of
ripe mammee apples. One by one, these burst open, and
thousands of tiny children tumbled to the ground. These
children danced around their tree-mother, then they ran
inside the house to rescue their mother's body. Their little
hands scraped the salt grains from her neck and dusted
her body down. Finally they carried her body out into the
garden and reattached her head.

Delighted, the mother chopped up the mammee tree
to make broomsticks, and she taught her children all
the helpful spells she knew. Then, together, they
chased her controlling husband far, far away.

CHAPTER 11

The Man Who Hunted Children

SOUTH AFRICA

nce there were two children. Their parents had died long ago, so they were used to looking after themselves. They took it in turns to do the chores and they bolted their door at night.

One day, rumours flew around their village. People said there was a man on the prowl who hunted children. They said he took them away in sacks and feasted upon their flesh.

'We must be careful,' said the sister. 'Brother, when you come back home, sing this song outside so I know it is you.'

She sang a song for him to memorise. It would have been a good idea, if the man who hunted children had not been right outside their house, listening to every word.

When the brother went to the market, the man came up to their door and knocked softly upon it.

'Sister, it is I!' he croaked. 'Let me sing you our song.'

He sang it in a deep, deep voice that resembled a lion.

'That is not my brother!' the sister laughed. 'You don't sound like him at all!'

The man vanished and came back in the morning.

'Sister, it is I!' he squeaked. 'Let me sing you our song.'

He sang it in a higher pitch but he sounded like a hyena.

'That is not my brother!' the sister snorted. 'You don't sound like him at all!'

The man fled and came back in the morning.

'Sister, it is I!' he whispered. 'Let me sing you our song.'

This time, the man wrapped his hands around his throat, squeezing it to shrink his voice box to the size of a young boy's. Then he sang the children's song.

'Brother, it is you!' The sister beamed and opened the door wide.

She did not have time to scream.

The man bundled her into a sack and dragged her out of the house. It was so dark inside that sack, and it was filled with the voices of dead children.

However, the reason the sister had not had time to scream was because she had reached behind her to grab a fistful of ashes from the fire. As she was pulled down the streets, far away from the village, she stuck her small hand out of the sack and let the ashes trail along the ground, in the hope her brother would be able to follow.

Indeed, when the brother returned at sunset, he guessed what had happened at once. He sprinted down the road after his clever sister, chasing the trail of ashes as it curved down to the river and into the night.

On the riverbank, the brother found the man who hunted children. He was sharpening his knife on a stone, crouched over a bone-white fire. When the man rose to his feet and walked away to collect more firewood, the brother dashed down to free his sister from the sack.

'We must run,' he whispered. 'Quick! Before he returns!'

'No,' said the sister. 'If we run, he will see the empty sack and he will chase us. We must fill it with something else.'

The sister had thought about this carefully. During her time in the sack, she had heard a constant buzzing and, sure enough, there was a beehive on the tree above them. The siblings tiptoed to it and gently took it down, tipping it into the empty sack.

Then they hid and they waited.

The man who hunted children came back with his firewood. He threw it onto the flames and the fire coughed into the sky.

'It's my dinner time, little one,' the man breathed, standing over the sack as he opened it wide.

The air was suddenly filled with a vicious hum: an army
of noise; a swarm of anger. The man screamed as the bees
flew out of the sack and stung him all over, again and again.
Thousands and thousands of them raging against him in
the dark.

'Now we can go,' the sister said, grinning. She took her
brother by the hand and the two of them hurried away
to safety.

Behind them, the man who hunted children howled and
dived headfirst into the river to try to sooth his stings. But
this was a mistake. You see, the river did not like this violent
man either. So when his body entered the water, the riverbed
reached up and grabbed him by the head. It pulled him
down and down, refusing to let go … slowly eating him
alive. His torso thrashed under the water, and his legs kicked
hopelessly in the night air above.

There was nothing the man could do.

His flailing limbs twitched in the moonlight, until
he slowly turned into a tree.

The Son of Seven Mothers

INDIA

here was once a king who wanted a child. He married one woman, then another, but still no child came. When the king had seven wives but no children, he wandered through the hills in frustration. As the sun began to set, a woman emerged from the trees. She smelled like a tiger, and her voice seemed to purr.

'Listen,' she said softly. 'I can tell you want a child. If you marry me and throw away your other wives, I promise you will have a son.'

The king was hypnotised.

He married the woman at once, and she became queen.

The king's seven wives were thrown into a deep well in the palace gardens. It was dank and full of echoes, like a galaxy in the ground.

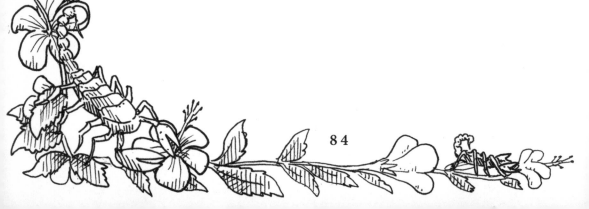

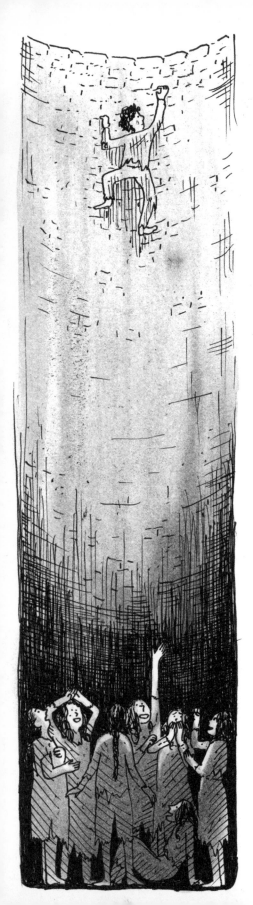

Over the coming months, the queen's promise was fulfilled – although not in the way the king had expected. When he threw his wives into that well, he didn't know they were all pregnant. One by one, the wives gave birth underground. They didn't have much food, and they were all very hungry, so they ate their newborn babies, munching on their bones.

Above ground, the oblivious king still waited for a son.

However, all was not lost, for one of the wives did not eat her baby. She cradled her son and nurtured him. She told him stories and sang him songs. As the years went by, he learned to climb like a mountain goat, and all the women encouraged him to reach up for the sun.

'Escape, dear child, and bring us food,' the wives said. 'Escape, into the world, and set yourself free.'

The small boy scampered up the walls of the well, his tiny fingers finding grips where his seven mothers could not. Finally, he reached the light.

He emerged into the gardens and ran to the palace. He
made friends with the chef, who hired him to sweep the floor.

'You're new,' said the queen when she first saw the boy.
'Where are you from?'

'I come from the well.' The boy grinned. 'My seven
mothers live there.'

The queen froze, realising she was speaking to a prince – a
prince who could take her crown, if he discovered who he was.

There was nothing for it – the queen would have to kill him.

'I need you to do me a favour, child,' she said smoothly.
'My favourite drink is bear milk, but we don't have any here.
Can you go and find a bear, and bring its milk to me?
I would be ever, ever so grateful.'

She flashed her perfect teeth, and the boy went merrily
on his way.

Out on his quest, he found a young girl practising archery.

'Where are you off to?' she asked, spearing an apple
to a tree.

The boy smiled. 'I'm going to collect bear milk for the
queen. She says it is her favourite drink.'

The girl frowned. She had heard of this evil queen and
knew the boy was being tricked.

'I saw the bears this morning,' she said coolly. 'They have
run out of milk. Go back to your queen and tell her she can't
have any today.'

The boy thanked the girl and ran back to the castle.

The queen's nostrils flared when she saw the boy had not been eaten by a bear.

'If there is no bear milk,' she snapped, 'fetch me the milk of a leopard. That's my second favourite drink.'

The boy set off again, and once more he saw the girl.

'Where are you off to?' she asked, looking up from her book.

'I'm going to collect leopard milk for the queen,' said the boy. 'She says it is her second favourite drink.'

The girl scowled. 'I saw the leopards yesterday,' she told him. 'They have gone away on holiday. Go and tell your queen she can't have any leopard milk today.'

The boy thanked the girl and hurried home.

The queen was livid.

'If there is no leopard milk,' she yelled, 'bring me the milk of a dragon – bring it to me now!'

The boy did not know where to find a dragon. He rushed back to the girl who seemed to know so much.

'The queen wants dragon milk,' he panted. 'Do you know where dragons live?'

The girl sighed.

She was tired of this terrible queen.

'Here,' she said, reaching into her pocket and pulling out a bottle of poison. 'This is a bottle of dragon milk. If you drink it and you have a human heart, it will fill you up with joy. But if you drink it and you have a tiger heart, scorpions will fall out of your mouth whenever you try to speak.'

The boy thanked her and sprinted back to the palace. The girl followed close behind to see what would happen next.

The boy hurtled into the dining room.

'I have your dragon milk, your majesty!'

The queen gaped, her fork halfway to her mouth. 'How on earth did you get that, child?'

'They say dragon milk will fill you with joy,' he said, hoping she'd be pleased.

The queen smirked. 'Joy, you say? Well, I suppose we could all do with some of that.'

The girl sneaked into the room just in time to see the queen gulping down the bottle of poison.

There was a brief pause.

The queen coughed and she spluttered.

She wheezed and she retched.

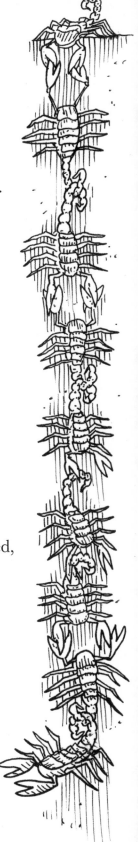

Then she grabbed her throat in horror as hundreds
of scorpions fell out of her mouth. They buried themselves
in her hair and scurried across the table. The queen
attempted to scream, but more scorpions blocked her throat.
They tumbled from her mouth in waves and covered the
palace floor.

The king wandered in bleary-eyed. 'What is all this
commotion?'

The queen ran past him in distress, out into the garden,
vomiting yet more scorpions across the sun-bleached grass.

Soon there were so many scorpions that they smothered
every surface. They invaded the flower beds and dug up
the soil. They littered the trees and swam in the pool.
Then they found a deep well and scuttled inside it.

When the scorpions discovered the seven mothers at the
bottom of that well, they examined them carefully. The
scorpions could hear their human hearts, so they decided
to help. They linked their tails to form a rope and slowly
pulled the mothers up. The women cheered as they emerged,
blinking in the sun.

'Will someone please tell me what is going on!' cried
the king.

The girl danced among the scorpions.

The son hugged his seven mothers.

And in a corner of the garden, the poisoned queen died.

CHAPTER 13

The Girl With the Horse's Head

CHINA

There was once a girl who loved her father very much, and she was extremely sad whenever he went away on business.

'You know,' she said to her horse, 'if you brought my father back, I'd be so grateful that I would marry you.'

Now, you might think that the horse couldn't understand her, but you would be wrong. The horse loved the girl – even more than the girl loved her father. So, upon hearing this, the horse reared up on his hind legs and ran out of the paddock, down the hill and onto the road, faster than if he'd had wings.

The girl watched him go, startled and confused.

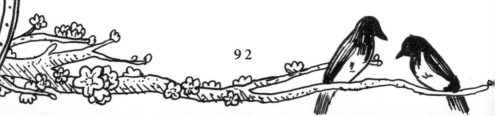

That evening, the horse
returned with the girl's father.
The man was panicked, thinking
something terrible must have happened
to have been dragged back home.

'What's the matter?' he asked, hugging his
daughter close.

'Oh, nothing,' she said, blushing. 'I just missed
you, that's all.'

The horse neighed and stamped the ground and
nibbled at her hair.

'Oh, Father,' the girl whispered. 'I promised the horse that
if he brought you home, I would marry him. But I don't want
to marry him. What should I do?'

Her father frowned and glared at the determined-looking
horse.

'Don't tell anyone about this,' he said. 'I will fix it.'

The father stayed up all night, pacing the kitchen. He had a
problem to solve. You see, if you promise to marry a horse,
you cannot undo that promise. The horse will follow you
everywhere. It will kick down your door. It will breathe in
your ear. It will force you to eat straw, even when you're full.

The father put his head in his hands. There was only
one thing he could do to save his beloved daughter. So he
sharpened his carving knife and slipped out into the yard.

The father did not enjoy killing the horse.

He enjoyed skinning him even less.

He buried the bones in the neighbouring field, away from his crops.

He hung the skin in the paddock, planning to turn it into a winter coat.

He did not speak about it to anyone.

A couple of weeks later, the daughter was walking by the paddock with a friend. She ran her hand along the white skin of the horse, saying, 'I can't believe that you tried to make me marry you. What a lucky escape I had!'

At these words, the horse skin jumped up and wrapped itself tightly around the daughter. Her friend screamed and ran home, calling out for help – but it was too late, for the horse skin lifted the daughter off her feet, and swept her away into the forest.

Soon, she was completely out of sight.

The villagers searched high and low for the missing daughter. They left gifts for the forest in the hope it would give her back. The father cried to the stars, but they would not show her face. Finally, when they were about to give up, they found her – still wrapped in the horse's skin, hanging from a tree, completely enclosed, like a human-sized fruit.

The horse's skin had turned into a silkworm cocoon, brilliant and silver. When the villagers cut it down and opened it up, the girl was curled inside it, and she had been transformed. Now she had a horse's head.

There were millions of moon-coloured threads covering her body – enough to make a thousand winter coats – and one of these was tied around her finger, like a wedding ring.

The Woman and the Glass Mountain

SPAIN

he leaves were falling, and the palace was having a party. Their princess had just turned one. Balloons filled the corridors, clowns tumbled down the stairs and all the townsfolk were invited. Everyone, that was, apart from the Warlock of the Mountain. It was bad form to forget to invite anyone, but it was especially terrible to forget to invite him.

As the king and queen paraded their daughter through the court, an icy gale howled down from the hills. Suddenly the warlock was upon them.

'You dare to forget me?' he hissed.

'My dear fellow,' the king hiccupped. 'Your invitation must have been stolen by the wind!'

The warlock did not believe him – which was fair enough, because it was a lie.

'You will be punished.' The warlock smiled.

He did not promise to prick the princess's finger with a spinning needle. He did not vow to put her to sleep for a hundred years. Instead, the warlock swiped his hand across the princess's head, and suddenly all her hair was gone. And not only her hair – the headband her grandmother had made vanished, too.

'When she's older, whichever suitor can retrieve her hair will deserve her hand in marriage,' the warlock announced. 'I'll keep it safe, for now.'

And with that, he was gone.

The queen cried. The king cried. The princess blinked at them, wondering what all the fuss was about.

'Everyone in the palace must hide their hair, so our princess never knows she is different!' ordered the king.

So it was that the princess grew up thinking that no one had hair growing out of their head. Until one day, when she was seventeen, the princess saw a woman delivering books to the palace. This woman didn't know about the no-hair rule, and the princess stared at the curls bouncing around her face.

'What is that?' the princess asked.

The woman grinned. 'It's just hair. What would you like to read?'

That evening, the princess and the woman talked about books. They spent many evenings together after that, too, reading aloud to each other in the palace library. They learned about haunted houses, sword fighting and flesh-eating zombies. They devoured each story by candlelight. Slowly, but surely, they began to fall in love.

'Daughter, it is your eighteenth birthday,' the king told the princess. 'And that means we must begin the quest for your hair.'

'Why?' she asked.

'It was stolen by the Warlock of the Mountain, my dear, and whoever should retrieve it is worthy of your hand in marriage.'

'But—' the princess began.

'Summon the princes!' the king cried, without listening to what his daughter was trying to say.

Letters were sent to suitors far and wide, and rumours of princes brave enough to face the Warlock of the Mountain rang through the streets.

'Do you actually want a suitor to get your hair back?' the woman asked the princess.

'Not really,' she sighed. 'I'm quite happy as I am. But there is one thing that I would like.'

'Name it.'

'My headband,' said the princess. 'My father says that was stolen, too. It was made by my grandmother, so I'd like to be reunited with that.'

'Okay.' The woman smiled, and kissed her goodnight.

Three princes arrived to embark on the king's quest, but they were not quite what everyone had in mind.

The first prince was only in it for the money. On his way to the mountain he stumbled across a goldmine that distracted him so much, he fell right to the bottom of it.

The second prince was also distracted. He walked halfway up the mountain and came across a lake. He paused and peered into it, staring at his own reflection, and he was so captivated that he tumbled into the water and was never seen again.

The third prince was a trickster. He didn't want to do any of the hard work himself, so he hired other people to do it for him, then he waited.

The woman did not wait. She wanted to retrieve the headband for her princess. So off she went.

The first obstacle she encountered was rather strange. Hedges rose out of the mist with no warning and surrounded her. A sign by the path said: 'Welcome to the land of evil spirits!' The woman could see the warlock's mountain beyond the fog, but she had no idea how to get to it. More hedges sprang up whichever way she turned, and ghostly figures prowled

the maze she now found herself inside.
They tapped her on the shoulder and
breathed on her neck.

'You are lost,' one of the ghosts
whispered. 'You will never get through.'

But the woman thought about all
the books she had read, and several of
them contained mazes. So she closed
her eyes and remembered everything
she had learned. Then she stepped
forward with purpose, again and again,
until the spiderwebbed hedges parted
and she reached the other side.

Now she was at the base of the mountain. It was made of blue glass and very difficult to climb, but she forced herself to try, scrambling up on her hands and knees.

After several days, the woman reached a river. It looked easy enough to cross, but as she crept closer to it, she swore she could hear the river laughing – or perhaps that was just the wind biting at her ears. The only way up was through the water, so the woman strode into the river's numbing depths.

'You are disturbing my mountain,' the river grumbled. 'This is no place for you.'

The water bubbled around her knees, then it rose into the air. It took on the face of the warlock and screamed like a banshee, crashing down upon the woman in the hope that she would drown.

But the woman thought about all the books she had read, and several of them contained rivers. So she closed her eyes and remembered everything she had learned. Then she swam wildly, her lungs burning with effort, until the vicious waves parted and she reached the other side.

When the woman neared the top of the mountain, she found herself in a garden of bluebells. They covered the ground like a blanket and made her feel very sleepy.

'Hello,' purred a voice. 'What have we here?'

The woman spun round and saw a maiden emerging from the flowers. She had hair that cascaded over her shoulders and fell all the way to the ground. It snaked across the grass, scattered with violet petals.

'Are you here for the princess's hair?' the maiden asked.

'I am here for her headband,' said the woman. 'It was made by her grandmother and now she wants it back.'

'What a shame,' the maiden said, pouting. 'Wouldn't you prefer to leave with me?'

'I am only interested in the princess,' said the woman, standing tall.

The maiden snarled. 'Then you must die.'

Suddenly, the maiden was no longer a maiden, she was a bear. Her teeth were ice picks, her fur matted with blood. She roared so fiercely that avalanches fell around them, crushing the bluebells and turning everything to snow.

The woman pulled her sword from its sheath and gulped. She had never fought a bear before. The beast launched itself at her, tearing at the air with its claws.

Surely this was the end.

THE WOMAN AND THE GLASS MOUNTAIN

But the woman thought about all the books she had read, and several of them contained dangerous bears. So she took a deep breath and remembered everything she had learned. She darted and she ducked. She ripped and she speared. She fought until the bear's fur parted and its heart crashed to the earth, and then the woman was able to continue on her way.

At the peak of the mountain, the woman found the princess's hair frozen in ice. She hacked at it until the frost shattered, and freed both the hair and the headband.

The ground beneath her began to tremble.

'Congratulations,' the warlock bellowed, though she couldn't see him. It seemed he was talking from within the mountain itself. 'Let me help you get down from my mountain.'

And before the woman could protest, the warlock had summoned an almighty gale. It swept her off her feet and caused her to tumble down the glass mountain. The wind tore at the hair in her hand and ripped it from her grasp, so that it flew off and fell somewhere out of sight.

CHAPTER 14

At the bottom of the mountain, the trickster prince waited. All the people he had hired had failed in their quest. He was vexed, and yet … a cold gust of wind zoomed by him, and to his great surprise the princess's hair landed squarely at his feet.

'Now we shall see who has won my daughter's hand!'
the king declared. He threw open the doors of the royal
court in the hope of revealing the three princes.

Only one stood there.

This prince looked neat and tidy, not a scratch on him,
for of course he hadn't gone up the mountain at all.

'Your majesty.' He bowed. 'I have brought your
daughter's hair.'

The trickster prince whipped it from his pocket with
a flourish and displayed the hair to all watching.

'Aha!' The king applauded. 'Well done! Daughter,
come and see this!'

The princess was ushered towards the prince. She nodded
politely and took the hair from him. 'Thank you, but this is
not what I wanted.' She turned to the king. 'And, Father,
I had already made my choice.'

The king spluttered. 'What do you mean, my dear?'

Another person tiptoed into the court. She was covered in
bruises, but she smiled broadly, and she held the princess's
headband aloft.

'I have brought you your grandmother's gift,' the woman
said. 'I was the one who ventured up the mountain.'

The princess flung herself at the woman, and everyone
in the court cheered at the sight of such happiness.

'Well, we'd best prepare for a celebration!' The king
beamed, joining in with the applause. 'I think the library
would be the perfect place for a wedding, don't you?'

So the princess and the woman were married. They lived
happily with many books, and they learned many things,
reciting stories by heart. Their favourite tales were the
gruesome ones, which they read aloud in the dark.

Afterword

JEN CAMPBELL

Fairy tales are slippery beasts, born thousands of years ago. Historically, they were told via word of mouth, which is why they often have repeating elements, making them easier to remember. People told them over fires, and in the royal courts, and they weren't just for children. They were for everyone. As they were spoken, the tales changed. They evolved like a creature: one storyteller would add one element, another would change something else.

As a result, we can find variations of the same tales all around the world. For instance, you may have realised that one of the tales in this book is a version of 'Hansel and Gretel'. As for other well-known fairy tales, one of the earliest versions of 'Cinderella' was called 'Ye Xian' and originated in China, first recorded in 850 AD. In that version, it's a magical fish, not a fairy godmother, who helps the girl escape

114

her awful family. Old versions of 'Snow White' have her
mother (not her stepmother) dancing on hot coals until she
dies. In some editions of 'Cinderella', her stepsisters cut off
their toes and heels to try to fit into that slipper. And as for
'The Little Mermaid' … well, in Hans Christian Andersen's
story she died. More recently – in the last two hundred years
– a lot of the gore has been removed from fairy tales to make
them less grisly for children. Here, I've put that gore back in.

I'm fascinated by the history of storytelling. In this book,
I've collected fourteen fairy tales from around the world and
retold them for you. Like any storyteller, I've changed certain
things to put my own stamp on them. In 'The Wife Who
Could Remove Her Head', the wife is not punished
for wanting to explore on her own as she is in other versions.
I turned the grandmother into a house in 'The Daughter
Who Loved a Skeleton' and a woman, not a man,
marries the princess in 'The Woman and the
Glass Mountain'.

AFTERWORD

While I love studying fairy tales, I dislike how often they present evil characters with disfigurements to 'show' the reader these characters should be feared. This is harmful and outdated and I especially feel this as someone with a disfigurement myself. This is why I am celebrating a princess with hair loss and a deaf man who happens to fall for a merman. In 'The Princess Who Ruled the Sea', a young woman who has her fingers cut off is not scorned or seen as monstrous. As someone with ectrodactyly (missing fingers), I wish I had seen more of these stories when I was growing up. I also wanted to push aside the stereotypical descriptions of women in traditional fairy tales: that they are beautiful or pretty, and almost never clever nor brave. So there is only one mention of the word 'beautiful' in this book, and when that word does appear, it is about a man.

I hope you had fun with these stories. I hope they scared you. I hope they tickled you. I hope they made you think about our strange little world.

If you'd like to leave my cabin in the forest now, the exit is just over there. I can show you the way out.

But if you'd like to stay, and read the book again, I can make us both a cup of tea.

Jen Campbell is a *Sunday Times* bestselling author
and award-winning poet. She is the author of ten
published books across non-fiction, poetry, short
stories and children's books. Her latest titles for
children include the *Franklin and Luna* series.
She specialises in the history of fairy tales
and the representation of disfigurement.

Find out more at www.jen-campbell.co.uk

Adam de Souza is an illustrator and cartoonist
who resides along the rainy coast of Vancouver,
Canada. He both writes and draws his own
comics as well as illustrates for clients such as
The Globe and Mail, VICE, and *The Reader's Digest.*

His work can be found at www.kumerish.com and
he is active on twitter and instagram @kumerish.